Baby Kangaroo

Written by Jill Eggleton
Illustrated by John Bennett

Rigby

Baby Kangaroo saw a spider.

5

Baby Kangaroo saw a mouse.

I am big.

Baby Kangaroo
saw a bird.

Baby Kangaroo saw a rabbit.

Baby Kangaroo
saw a crocodile.

13

A Comparison Chart

▬▬▬ **Guide Notes**

Title: Baby Kangaroo

Stage: Emergent – Magenta

Genre: Fiction

Approach: Guided Reading

Processes: Thinking Critically, Exploring Language, Processing Information

Written and Visual Focus: Comparison Chart

READING THE TEXT

Tell the children that the story is about a baby kangaroo who thinks it is too big to be in a pouch.

Talk to them about what is on the front cover. Read the title and the author / illustrator.

"Walk" through the book, focusing on the illustrations and talking to the children about the animals that the baby kangaroo meets and how it thinks it is much bigger than them.

Before looking at pages 12 - 13, ask the children to make a prediction.

Read the text together.

THINKING CRITICALLY
(sample questions)

• Why do you think the baby kangaroo wanted to get out of the pouch?
• Do you think the baby kangaroo is big enough to be out of its pouch after all?

EXPLORING LANGUAGE
(ideas for selection)

Terminology
Title, cover, author, illustrator, illustrations

Vocabulary
Interest words: kangaroo, spider, bird, mouse, rabbit, crocodile
High-frequency words: I, am, saw, a

Print Conventions
Capital letter for sentence beginnings and names (**B**aby **K**angaroo), periods